Croc by the Rock

ReadZone Books Limited

50 Godfrey Avenue
Twickenham
TW2 7PF
UK

For Charlotte and Samuel

First published in this edition 2014

© in this edition ReadZone Books Limited 2014
© in text Hilary Robinson 2005
© in illustrations Mike Gordon 2005

Hilary Robinson has asserted her right under the Copyright Designs and Patents Act 1988 to be identified as the author of this work.

Mike Gordon has asserted his right under the Copyright Designs and Patents Act 1988 to be identified as the illustrator of this work.

Every attempt has been made by the Publisher to secure appropriate permissions for material reproduced in this book. If there has been any oversight we will be happy to rectify the situation in future editions or reprints. Written submissions should be made to the Publisher.

British Library Cataloguing in Publication Data (CIP) is available for this title.

Printed in Malta by Melita Press

ISBN 978 1 78322 143 1

Visit our website: www.readzonebooks.com

Croc by the Rock

by Hilary Robinson
illustrated by Mike Gordon

READZONE

When Jake took his net...

...to fish by the rock

6

he saw what he thought...

...was the eye of a croc!

10

"A croc by the rock!"
Jake called to the man...

...who let his dog out

from the back of a van.

The dog stretched his paws

then raced round the rock...

...then jumped in the lake

to hunt for the croc!

He dipped and he dived

as the kids rushed to take...

...some photographs of

the croc in the lake.

Then everyone cheered

as the dog showed to all...

...that the crocodile's eye

was only a ball!

But later that day

Jake fished on the rock...

...and found in his net...

...a tooth from a croc!

Did you enjoy this book?

Look out for more *Redstarts* titles — first rhyming stories

Alien Tale by Christine Moorcroft and Cinza Battistel
ISBN 978 1 78322 135 6

A Mouse in the House by Vivian French and Tim Archbold
ISBN 978 1 78322 416 6

Batty Betty's Spells by Hilary Robinson and Belinda Worsley
ISBN 978 1 78322 136 3

Croc by the Rock by Hilary Robinson and Mike Gordon
ISBN 978 1 78322 143 1

Now, Now Brown Cow! by Christine Moorcroft and Tim Archbold
ISBN 978 1 78322 132 5

Old Joe Rowan by Christine Moorcroft and Elisabeth Eudes-Pascal
ISBN 978 1 78322 138 7

Pear Under the Stairs by Christine Moorcroft and Lisa Williams
ISBN 978 1 78322 137 0

Pie in the Sky by Christine Moorcroft and Fabiano Fiorin
ISBN 978 1 78322 134 9

Pig in Love by Vivian French and Tim Archbold
ISBN 978 1 78322 142 4

Tall Story by Christine Moorcroft and Neil Boyce
ISBN 978 1 78322 141 7

The Cat in the Coat by Vivian French and Alison Bartlett
ISBN 978 1 78322 140 0

Tuva by Nick Gowar and Tone Erikson
ISBN 978 1 78322 139 4